For Ollie,
with my love,

Michael

michael morpurgo
Carnival of the Animals

First published in Great Britain by
HarperCollins *Children's Books* in 2021
HarperCollins *Children's Books* is a division of
HarperCollins*Publishers* Ltd
1 London Bridge Street
London SE1 9GF

www.harpercollins.co.uk

HarperCollins*Publishers*
1st Floor, Watermarque Building, Ringsend Road
Dublin 4, Ireland

1

ISBN 978-0-00-845982-6

michael morpurgo
Carnival of the Animals

A WHOLE NEW WORLD OF ANIMAL POEMS

Illustrated by
MICHAEL FOREMAN

HarperCollins *Children's Books*

Contents

Overture

Just to say that in amongst these *Carnival of the Animals* poems I have written, you'll come across the name Saint-Saëns. And in case you don't know, Camille Saint-Saëns is a great composer who lived a while ago now, and he wrote some wonderful music with animals in mind, a whole carnival of animals.

So, because I love the music I wrote some poems to go with it. So we could make a concert together, him and me. That's why you'll find his name, which is as difficult to spell and pronounce as mine, in some of the poems.

Then when I was writing the poems for the carnival of this Saint-Saëns – pronounced SAN SONS, by the way – I got so excited that I decided to write about lots more animals. So our carnival became bigger, louder, so big and so loud that it can be heard all over the world. And so we made a book. Hope you like it. And listen to his music – you'll love it. And you'll love Michael Foreman's lovely pictures too. He's painted almost the whole world, and so many animals. Count and see how many!

And if you look very hard, you might notice in some of the pictures a people animal, one of us, like you and me, living amongst them, singing and dancing with them, all of us joining in the carnival of the animals, to celebrate the world, to celebrate our existence on this precious planet of ours.

Michael Morpurgo

CARNIVAL OF THE ANIMALS

Part One

Lion

I told this Saint-Saëns fellow straight.

I'm the king, right? If you're going to

Compose this *Carnival of the Animals*,

And you want me to be part of it,

That's fine. But I get to come on first,

Strut my stuff, shake out my mane for the people.

And I get the main part in this thing.

I'm the star, right, Monsieur Saint-Saëns?

No lion, no concert, no nothing.

You hear me? And make your music

Fit for a king, you hear? Or I just might eat you.

And not too loud. I've got some sleeping to do.

Hens AND Roosters

I've been doing a lot of thinking lately.

Pecking about is fine; it's got to be done.

But it doesn't improve the mind.

Thinking does, and music. Which is why

I warble a lot, chuckle a lot – we all do. Keeps us happy.

But that's what I've been thinking about. Happiness.

It's a right, right? The pursuit of happiness.

I mean, what have we got to be happy about?

We lay our eggs, and they just take them away. Mostly.

And that rooster who fancies himself rotten

Wakes us up every morning with his infernal cock-a-doodle-dooing.

And then there's the fox. Always out there watching, waiting.

You know what makes me happy? A chick to come pecking with me.

I'd like that, like that very much. A chick that cheeps, musically.

Wild Donkeys,

SWIFT ANIMALS

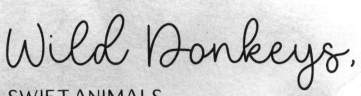

None of you have ever seen a wild donkey.

I am wild. I am free. I run through snow and over mountains.

I run through sand and over deserts.

I have feet that have clambered all over the world.

I have ears that hear all the music in the world.

I have a head large with brain

And a heart full of courage.

I am the Ulysses of animals, the Achilles.

No one catches me, not by the heel, not by the mane.

I don't need a mane to brag to the world.

I bray. I'm nobody's ass, no one's slave.

I'm donkey wild, donkey free.

And, unlike Lion, I've a cross on my back.

Make what you like of that.

Tortoises

You people are obsessed with speed. You know you are.
You know the fable? Well, of course you do.
The hare with the speed ego took a nap, and I won.
But what the hare didn't know, nor La Fontaine,
Was that I don't like racing, don't see the point of it.
I'm happy, we're happy, being slow.
And slow is good. Slow is cool.
Imagine a world where we all go slow.
No need to wish for cars or trains or planes.
Imagine an Olympics where the slowest wins.
Tortoises on every winners' podium, gold medals round our necks.
And no need to build any more houses. We carry ours with us.
And we're still here after millions and squillions of years.
You may worship speed, but you'll wear yourselves out.
We never do. We never have.
Take it easy. Go slow, and you'll go happy.
Take it from a tortoise.

Elephant

My child once looked up at me and asked:
"Why do you cry, Mama?"
"Because sometimes I am sad," I told her.
"But why are you sad?" she asked.
"Because you are so small and beautiful,
And I love you more than I can say."
"Will I cry too when I am older, Mama?"
"I hope so. And I hope you will laugh too."
"Will you show me how to laugh, Mama?"
"I will show you," I replied. "I will show you everything."
When I trumpeted my love and my laughter all over the savannah,
The grasses and trees shivered with joy,
And so did my child.

Kangaroos

I'm not just a hopper, you know. I'm not a flipping flea, you know.

I'm not a jumper or a leaper or a springer neither.

I'm a k-k-k-k-k-kangaroo. And proud of it, proud of it.

I'm a lurruper if you want to know.

Me and my kind have been lurruping around all over Australia
Before it was even Australia, before men came and bothered us,
And chased us and hunted us.
We were here first. And we are still here.
And we're not going anywhere.

You might think all we do is jump.
We don't. We dance, we sing, we thump.
The rhythm section of the outback,
We make the music of our world.
Hear how we play.

Aquarium
(OR, I HAVE A FRIEND)

I don't like it in here. It's too quiet.

I'm a tigerfish, and the others won't come near me.

What do they think I am, a shark?

In the sea where I came from,

I could hear wave-song and whale-song,

Watch seaweed dance, feel the thunder and roar

Of storms above. And I had my family and my friends.

Went to school with them, played with them.

We had the seas to explore, whole wide oceans.

Not a glass tank. A twitch of my tail

And I have circumnavigated my entire globe.

But I have a face who comes to gaze at me

From the other side. A little face who sings to me.

I can just hear it, like a distant whale-song,

And that makes me happy again.

I have a friend. She has a friend.

All is well.

Long-eared CHARACTERS

I'm all ears –

I can hear you thinking it.

Well, I'm not a bat – I don't hang about upside down.

You're thinking I must be an owl.

No, I'm not an owl. No feathers, don't tu-whit or -whoo.

You're thinking I must be a rabbit or a hare or a fox.

No, none of these. I'm me.

I am a donkey, not a wild jackass idiot donkey,

But a proper working donkey.

I can carry twenty times my own weight,

Put up with all your curses and your whips and sticks,

Put up with the flies. I just walk on, work on.

And when I'm tired and lonely, I sing.

I'm not all ears. I'm more than that.

I am a singer, a diva.

I bray and the whole world hears me, knows it's me.

I make you hear me.

So you don't dare think I'm all ears.

The Cuckoo

IN THE DEPTHS OF A WOOD

It's a long-haul flight, I'm telling you. Cuckoo!
But a cuckoo has to cuckoo, if you see what I'm saying. Cuckoo!
Even if we have to travel. Cuckoo!
And it's worth it when we get there. Cuckoo!

The people love my song, listen for it, echo it back. Cuckoo!
Must be spring, they say. How they love my song. Cuckoo!
Cuckoo, I call, from the dark of the woods, over the bright fields. Cuckoo!
Down the swirling river, over the whispering reeds. Cuckoo!

I'll lay my egg in some lucky warbler's nest. Cuckoo!

Small nest, big egg. Lovely little bird, a warbler. Cuckoo!
But not the brightest. Cuckoo!
They'll feed my little cuckoo all he can swallow. Cuckoo!
Work themselves to death. Cuckoo!
Grow my chick into a giant. Cuckoo!
No little warbler siblings allowed. Cuckoo!

Job done. Home again.
Cuckoo!

Aviary

(OR, THE SONG OF OUR DREAMS)

We like it in our aviary. No, honestly, we do mostly.

We chirrup and flutter and sing on our perches.

Don't pity us – we're used to it.

Because we have forgotten.

Forget freedom for long enough,

And you forget you had it once.

Linnet and Lark and Finch and Canary,
We're all here, all good friends.
But then they bring us a new one,
Bright and new from the jungle
With strong wild wings,
And with stories that stir memories,
Dreams of a world lost to us for ever,
That remind us of the chorus, the carnival,
The freedom we once had.
Then we sing of our dreams.
Remember the carnival
And we can live again.

Pianists

(OR, WHO SINGS BEST IN THE BATH?)

You think this is easy, to make a carnival,

And a carnival of animals, Monsieur Saint-Saëns?

All this scratching and scraping, banging and blowing?

And all these wretched keys to choose from?

All the practice, all those rehearsals?

And as for that conductor!

Without even thinking, without rehearsal, without conductor,

The birds do it, the bees do it,

Even educated elephants do it.

Does Lion have to rehearse his roaring?

We know Donkey does not practise her braying.

Do I have to do my scales to sing in the bath?

Now which animal do you think
Sings best in the bath, I wonder?
Hippopotamus, in all that glorious mud?
No, Whale. Whale in the deep sings for all of us.
Oh, to make our instruments sing like a whale.
With no conductor! And no rehearsal!

Fossils

(OR, DOING THE BRONTOSAURUS)

Saint-Saëns would have loved it,

His *Carnival of the Animals* played in the museum,

And in the audience, Brontosaurus and us.

We sit there, looking up as we listen.

Watching him listen, wishing he was, hoping he was,

All of us willing him living and breathing.

And then, do not scoff, we see him swaying to the sound,
Moving to the music. His feet bones tapping,
His leg bones, his hip bones, his body bones,
His tail bones, his neck bones, his head bones.
He's shaking it all about, doing the brontosaurus.
And now we are too, on our feet and dancing with him.
A carnival of happy bones.

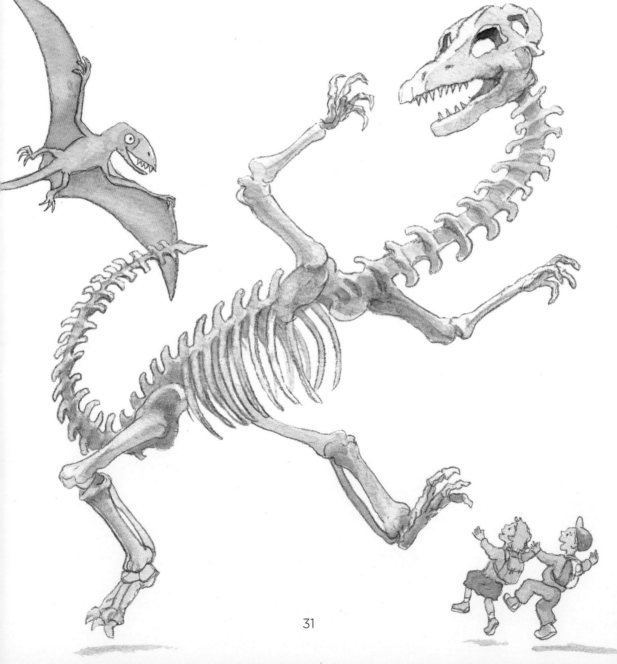

Swan

I am serene. I am silent. I am Swan.
I do not swim – I glide. I do not fly – I float.
Air and water are all the same to me.
You are all the same to me.
And I am the swan you want me to be.

I will be swan on the lake for all of you.
I will preen. I will dance. I will raise me up and beat my wings.
I will sing with my wings the sweetest song.
I will land impossibly, gracefully.
I will arch my neck. I will be beautiful for you.
I am beautiful for I am Swan.

But beware and take care.
Come too close with my family following on,
And I can be swift to anger.
Then I am swift to be wild, my wild self again.

But for now I am the swan you want me to be.
Speechless.
Listen to my silence.

The Finale

Merci, Monsieur Saint-Saëns, for your glorious *Carnival of Animals*.
Merci aussi, thanks too, to the animals who invited us to come.
We've loved being with you and with the band.

Or is it an orchestra? I don't care.

You play like a dream, made our dream,

Lived it with us.

Long live our lions and hens and tortoises and donkeys

And swans and elephants and kangaroos

And fish and birds, even cuckoos,

And musicians, even conductors,

And long live us!

Et vive Monsieur Saint-Saëns!

Our great carnival-maker, carnival-creator!

And, dear listeners, dear readers, *vive vous* too!

Second Overture

I wrote these next few poems because, by mistake, I'd left some animals out of the first part, and they told me they weren't at all pleased about it. So here are some more poems – just to keep them (and you) happy.

Everyone should be happy at a carnival.

Michael Morpurgo

CARNIVAL
OF THE ANIMALS

Part Two

Two Giraffes IN A ZOO

I hear what you're saying:
"Giraffes. Tall and near the sky.
Look how they lope.
They're funny, Mummy."

And you can stop your staring.

Got to say, you got us wrong.
You do me wrong too.
I don't lope. I float when I run.
And I do not belong in your zoo.

And you can stop your pointing too.

I belong under African sky,
With lions and leopards, elephants and wildebeest.
I've never been there – I was born here, in the zoo.
But I know the stories. And I am sad.
I know the stories my mama tells me:
"Once we were small not tall,
No bigger than a warthog.
But prettier though," my mama says.

"Small not good, pretty no use,
Easy prey for hyena and cheetah and lion.
Leaves and fruit grew high,
Too high to reach."

"So we giraffes grew too, only thing to do,
Grew our legs, our backs, our necks,
Faster to run, stronger to fight, taller to reach.
Thousands of years of growing tall we did," my mama says.

"Now we stride about, roam all over Africa.
Too hot, too cold, too wet, too dry maybe. But free.
We can reach the highest tree.
We can neck-whack away Lion and Hyena.

"No other animal is higher,
None more gentle and kind.
Be proud of being giraffe, my son.
Be glad, not sad, my son."

"But, Mama, will we ever be free?"
She does not answer me.
It is hard to be glad. I am in a zoo,
But my heart is in Africa.

I told you, you can stop your staring.
And you can stop your pointing too.
It's rude.
Or didn't your mama tell you?

Snow Leopard

I think you should know, you people.
We snow leopards, we know snow – we know mountains.
We live here, hide here, climb here, hunt here.
So we know you are waiting, watching.
It is our world, and you may not like to hear this.
You are not welcome here.
We like to be left alone.

Please go.

You two-legged people, you come up here
To catch a ghostly glimpse, to ooh and aah and wonder.
And why? Because we live so high, because we are so few.
But why so high, why so few?
Because you came and you drove us up high.
Because you came and you captured,
And you killed. You think we do not remember?

Still you come, maybe not with guns,
But with crampons and ropes and goggles.
You paparazzi people, you stalk us, lie in wait for us.
You hunt us down with your cameras.
Just leave us be, why don't you?
We like to be alone. I want to be alone.

We are made for here – you are not.
This is our home, not yours.
The mountains tempt you, trick you, freeze you.
We see you often, fallen and frozen, in your ropes and crampons.
You leave yourself behind,
Lie here for ever, bones blanched as snow.

But still you come to see if you can spot
A spotted me, a white and grey ghost,
In a land of grey and white,
My land, our land.
Just leave us be, why don't you?
We like to be alone. I want to be alone.

Please go away.

Narwhal

Listen. I've got a point to make.

Let's get one thing clear here:
I am in no way related to a unicorn.
No way, José! I am not pretty or
  pink or prancing.
All we have in common is a horn,
And mine is far longer and more
  beautiful,
And, much more importantly, mine
  is no adornment.
Mine is real. I am real.

This is the point I want you to
  understand.
A unicorn, like his horn, is a fake, a
  fiction, a fraud.

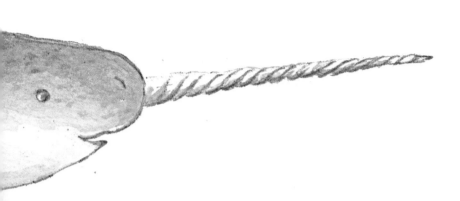

I am a narwhal. I am living. I have a proper horn,
A spiralling beautiful pointed ivory horn of my very own.

Sorry to say this, folks,
I know it's upsetting, but just get used to it.
There's no such thing as a unicorn.
You can find a unicorn only in poems or stories.
A horse with a horn! You cannot be serious.
A unicorn is a joke, but a serious joke, a troublesome one.

Trouble is, and it's a troubling trouble to me:
All the world knows a unicorn, loves a unicorn.
Bright white or pretty pink, they are adorable and sweet.

They are whatever you like to think they are,
Whatever you like to hope they are.
The more we hope, the more we believe.
You have to believe that.

You may believe in unicorns,
But do you know about narwhals?
Do you believe in us,
Deep in our cold blue waters of the north?
Do you know how for hundreds of years
We have been nothing to you but meat and oil and hide –
And horns?
Believe that, please, because it is true.

Believe how you loved our horns.
How kings and princes treasured them,
How the world wondered at them.
And out of these wonders, out of our horns, came the stories,
Stories – yes, you've guessed it –
Of those pretty pink prancing unicorns.

Just so you know then,
I'm telling you, there'd be no unicorns,

Not in stories, not even in pictures or poems,
Without narwhals.
Without us, without me,
Without my amazingly wonderful beautiful spiralling horn.

I've made my point.
OK?

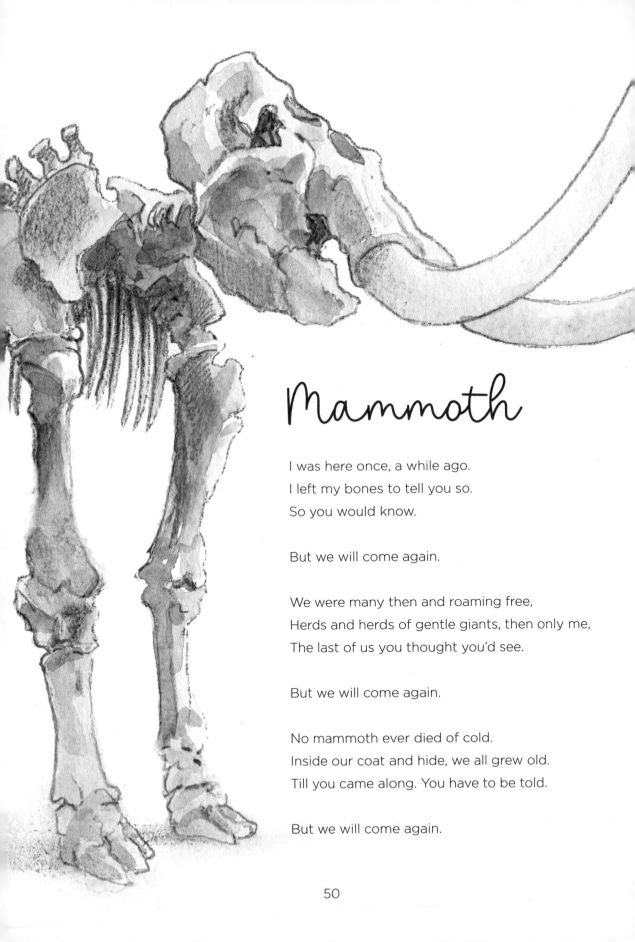

Mammoth

I was here once, a while ago.
I left my bones to tell you so.
So you would know.

But we will come again.

We were many then and roaming free,
Herds and herds of gentle giants, then only me,
The last of us you thought you'd see.

But we will come again.

No mammoth ever died of cold.
Inside our coat and hide, we all grew old.
Till you came along. You have to be told.

But we will come again.

The ice retreated, and mammoth met man.
No wolf can kill as well as you can.
How we fought, and how we ran.

But we will come again.

In my permafrost grave I lay and I lay
Till you dug me out and took me away,
Enough of me left, I heard you say.

I really will be coming again.

They've made me out of my DNA,
A newborn mammoth, my first new day.
Putting the world to rights, you say!
About time too, I say!

Hooray! Hooray!

Mammoth is becoming again.

Flamingo

Pink, candyfloss pink.

I mean, be honest, just think.

How would you like to be me?

Look down in the water and what do I see?

Bright pink, pink all over, every feather of me.

Did you know, and this is weird,
The pinker you are – no, it's really true –
The more other flamingos admire you?
But we all have a problem with our bill,
Or beak or nose, call it what you will.

It's gross, it's gruesome, it's gargantuan,
An inconvenient aberration.
You try eating with that thing, and drinking too.
And have you seen our knees?
Put on the wrong way, if you please.

And whoever did the engineering
Did not think of the take-off or the steering.
A duck just does it, a quacking lift-off, easy-peasy.
With us it's such a frantic paddling palaver,
And as for landing, you just want to get it over.

But look up there, look – can you see us now?
What a sight, what a wow!
Hundreds of us, all together, pink and proud of it,
Wide wings singing. See how I go, hear how I go.
I'm a happily honking frabjous flamingo.

Rhinoceroses

We are only just plural.
And some of us, our dear northern cousins,
Are no longer even singular.
Almost mammoths we are, but not quite.

Old as mammoths, old as the hills.
And we look it too, not ugly, just unlikely,
Every single one of us,
A million aeons old.

My skin is prehistoric parchment;
Our story written deep into every fold,
And armour too against arrow and spear.
We had no fear of leopard's tooth nor lion's claw.

Oh, I was invincible, once.
One snorting charge and I can scatter
My enemies far and wide –
Any pride of lions, any pack of hyenas.

I am a scattering battering ram.
But I have an Achilles nose,
A horny bump, a problematic protrusion.
My weapon of war has a weakness, a flaw.

Cut it off and grind it down,
Take it daily and you live for ever –
Some of you would believe anything,
My Achilles nose ground down for your longevity.

My nose is so special, so prized, so perfect for
A unique horn handle for your unique curved knife.
Rhino horn is better, more prestigious, you believe.
So shoot me dead and cut off my nose.

What sad and stupid and cruel people you are.
Can you not see? When you have used us all up,
What will there be? Just you, alone on the Earth.
And we will be like our dear northern cousins,

Rhinoceroses only in photograph or film,
Found only in your knives and stories and poems. Gone.
Gone then, gone for good.
Too late for tears, too late for us.

Oh, you will have your temporary longevity.
Oh, you will have our noses for your knives.
Oh, you will have the whole wide world to yourselves.
I hope it makes you happy.

The River AND Me

Now you see me. Now you don't.
A swimming bird, a flying fish,
A smart little dipper,
That's me.

Watch and you'll see me.
Blink and you won't.
Eyes wide open, wait, and I'll come.
That's me!

I'm a leaper, a white-bibbed bobber,
The jolliest jigger and shaker in the river,
Underwater, in the air, on my stone.
That's me.

Oh yes, and I can sing too,
In tune with the flow.
I'm a dancing, singing, carnival bird.
That's me.

And I'm not alone in my river.
Heron is here in the shallows, a still, grey ghost,
No friend of eels and frogs,
But a friend of mine.

He aarks when he's happy,
Aarks when he's angry.
Not easy to know what he's thinking,
But a very good friend of mine.

Kingfisher is almost gone before he was there.
I see him come and I see him go, just.
But oh, when he comes my way,
How he brightens my day.

He's the one they come to see.
Deep in your hides, the cameras wait.
Kingfisher sits there and poses.
How he brightens your day.

But what is it with ducks?

Why must they quack so horribly loud?

Always all at once too, making such a splash and fuss,

As they take off and fly.

And what do they do?

Disturb the whole sky,

Circle around and come right back,

And land where they started with a quackety-quack.

Look out for otters. If looks could kill,

We dippers always say.

They rule in this river,

And all of us are prey.

Salmon or sea trout, stickleback or shrimp,

All easy pickings for otters, the rotters.

Water rat or vole, ducklings, and yes, even dippers.

Not fussy, an otter, you swift and silent killer.

I love to watch the river drinkers,
The slurpers and the dribblers and the lappers.
They none of them see me.
Too busy emptying the river.

The cows come down in crowds.
They like to meander, to drink, to burp and . . .
Well wouldn't you know?
They gather for a while, just stand, just there cooling.

I miss them when they're gone.
A deer now, a tentative tread, ears pricking.
She's worried. They're always worried.
Think they must have crocodiles in their heads.

She startles now and springs away.
Dog comes, nose to the ground.
Lapping loud, busily, in a hurry.
Always in a hurry. Off again, tail whirling, gone.

My river is our river.
It goes without saying.
That's the good thing about river creatures –
We know it goes without saying.

Camel

I am Camel.
I spit on you because
You sit on me.

You think that's all I'm useful for?
You think I don't think.
I know this is all about drink.
I am Camel, and I spit on you.

Three days you can go without water.
For me, nine months is a doddle.

Water is for wimps – you get my meaning?
Who needs a wadi or oasis or well?
I am Camel, and I spit on you.

And as for you, great sun above,
Shine on, beat down, do your very worst.
You think you bother me?
Your heat is meat and drink to me.
I simply soak you in.
I am Camel. I spit on you too.

"Yaah! Yaah! Hut! hut!"
Is all I ever hear you say.

Tell me, who is doing all the walking?

And tell me too,
Who is crossing this desert for you?
Hard for you up there, just sitting?
Hut hut, yourself! Hut off!
I am Camel, and I spit on you.

You call me a ship of the desert.
I'm nobody's ship, you hear me?
Nobody's fool, I promise you.
Nobody's beast of burden either.
I'm thinker and poet,
Philosopher and traveller.
I have heart and mind and hope.
I am Camel, and I spit on you.

I am Camel.
I spit on you because
You sit on me.

Panda AND Orang-utan

We have never met till now.
Icons you might think we are, mere logos.
Not so, not so.

We wish to make a joint declaration
To the world, to you.
Just so you know.
We are celebrating existence.
That's what this carnival is for.
But there's more.
We are insisting on existence.
Rebelling against extinction.

We know why you see us as you do.
We have worked it out.
It's because we are few – because of you.
Because there's one of us who could be you,
And the other so soft you'd like a cuddle.

I am Orang-utan, not you. I live in trees.
I'm the gardener of the rainforest,
Take away my forest and I'm no more.
No trees, no bed, no fruit, no me.

I'm Panda. Happy enough to roam alone.
No cuddles needed or required, please.
All I want, all I need, is forests too.
Of bamboo. Oh yes, and solitude.
Do you think you could manage that?

And me, I'm a climber, a loose-limbed swinger,
Living the life in my canopy in the skies.
Leave me be.

And me? I'm happy when I'm hiding,
Unseen in bamboo hills of home, undisturbed.
Leave me be.
We trouble no one. So don't trouble us.

Tiger

Can a tiger change his stripes?
Come out of the shadows, out of the wild?
Can we be who we are not,
Sheathe our claws and swallow our roars?
Born to hunt. Born to be wild.
Or must I be?

Why am I a fearsome stalker?
Must I chase and kill my prey?
Can I not change familiar ways?
Eat berries and fruit, and why not cake?
Born to hunt. Born to be wild.
Or must I be?

You live your lives in dread of me –
Deer and Boar and Monkey and you.
And I live my life in dread of you too.
Why has it always been like this?
Born to hunt. Born to be wild.
Or must I be?

I had this idea in my dream last night,
A perfect solution, a resolution.
We both give up the killing and hunting.
No more will I be prey to you, nor you to me.
Born to hunt. Born to be wild.
Or must I be?

Is it a deal, a win-win deal for evermore?
I'd walk your streets. You'd walk my forests.
We'd talk and roar and walk together.
I'd even come to your house for tea.
Born to eat cake. Born to be wild.
Oh please, can I have my cake and eat it?

Animal Farm

(OR, WE WORK FOR A LIVING)

You Fox and Deer, you Rabbit and Hare,
Squirrel and Mouse, Pigeon and Rat,
Badger and Otter, Buzzard and Blackbird,
Don't you dare look down on us.
We work for a living!

Me most of all. I'm the barking one.

I do the driving and the gathering –
I'm the eyes and ears of animal farm –
The guarding and the ratcatching.
I'm the boss and the dogsbody round here.
And I work for a living!

Take my beautiful cows. I'm proud of them.
They don't just wander about and moo, you know.
They give up a calf every year.
They don't just lie there and regurgitate.
They give down their milk day after day.
They work for a living.

And take my wonderful sheep, my flock, my lovelies,
Out there in the winter snow, in the summer heat,
The gentlest mothers in all the world.
Not silly at all. Oh no, they know
What and who they're doing it for.
But they work for a living.

And all my happy hens and geese and ducks,

With all their chortling and honking and quacking,
They know their eggs go missing – they do.
They know and understand the score
And keep their peckers up, somehow.
They all work for a living too.

You think us fools? You think we are idiots?
We do what we have to do, that's all.
To be wild like you and free as air,
That's our dearest nightly dream.
Sun and truth dawn every morning.
We have to work for a living, not like you.

You sing your bright chorus, you fly your blue sky,
Sleep safe in your burrows and wander your woods.
Enjoy your hunting, and may you live long.
Only think more kindly of us down on our farm –
Not slaves, nor traitors, nor collaborators.
Remember always: we work for a living.

And as for him and as for her,
For all of them living up in the house,
They're farmers just like us.
We're family too, sort of.
We all look after each other.
They work for a living too, sort of.

Snow Bear

I am Snow Bear. I am Sea Bear. I am White Bear.
I wander far and wide,
Queen in my wild white kingdom.

I scent seal. I like seal. I follow my nose.
Come along, little ones – keep up, keep up.
If I can eat, you can live. Simple as that.

Tread soft like me. Go slow like me.
Not a sound, you hear? Now wait and watch.
Watch and learn. Your day will come, my babies.

A seal is wary. It's a waiting game.
He feels you coming – with his whiskery antennae.
He'll be gone like that, quick as a twick.

My nose is my sharpest weapon,
Better by far than jaws or claws.
I hide in my stillness, in my whiteness.

So it's his whiskers against my nose.
He wins most often. Get used to it.
If at first you don't succeed . . .

You will succeed. Believe it and you will.
Wait. Be still, my children. Feel him down there.
Pounce like a fox! Crash through the snow!

And look! We have what we came for.
Not a big one maybe, but a seal all the same.
"Enough is as good as a feast,"

As my mother would say to me.
Now drink, my babies, drink deep and long.
I killed for you. Now you live for me.

Bee

Behold the humble bumblebee.
That's me.

Oh, we do more than make you honey.
Bethink and believe you me.
Just bethink what you would live without.

Berries and cherries, and apples and pears,
Every fruit you can bethink of or see,
How can you bethink they grow there without me?

What of the flowers that bloom in the spring?
They happen by accident? Is that what you bethink?
Every flower you smell, every fruit you eat, that's me.

We bees are the pollinators of the planet.
We feed you all you need, all that's good.
Not burgers maybe, but broccoli we do. No, really we do.

Without us bees, the wise bethinker Einstein once said,
You people, you honey-thieving people,
Would have just four years of food left to live. Bethink on that.

Please do enjoy our honey, but try to remember:
Never persecute your pollinators. It is not wise or kind.
So you can keep your pesky pesticides just for yourselves.

Eat your fruit and all you should, but please bethink,
My dear good friends, bees do more than buzz.
We feed the world, feed you and yours.

We don't want a please; we don't need a thank-you.
Just open a window when we want to get out
And don't sit on us. We don't like it.

Behold the humble bumblebee.
That's me.

Man's Best Friend,

I AM

I just want to say, to neigh it out loud:
We were always man's best friend,
Woman's even more, by the way.

Dog was nothing but wild and wolf,
A howling hunting hit-dog –
No friend to man nor beast.

As for Cat, she sat on no mats or laps
But killed instead for fun, for food.
She taunted and teased,
she played with her prey.

Horse never lived to kill, nor killed to live.
We live for love; we live for you.
Always have done; always will.

You ride because we like you to.
We walk and trot and canter and gallop,
Whatever you like, whenever you like.

We've ploughed for you and mown for you,
Raced for you and jumped for you,
Gone to war, been killed for you.

We have been your friend indeed,
And you have been our friend in need.
Lived and loved our lives together.

So I say and neigh it again:
Horse is man's best friend, and woman's too.
You know I'm telling you true.

LAST WORD TO
Blackbird

S'cuse me!

Hey you,
down there,
Poet man,
in your wellies and your hat.
Yes, you!
You,
Picking your kale.
Up here, I'm up here,
Up in my tree.
See me?
Hear me?
Or have you forgotten me?
I'm not a snorer
Nor a grunter,
Don't bleat or bray
Or bellow.

I sing.

I sing like a bird.

I sing at dawn, every dawn.

I wake you; I wake the world.

I'm the diva of them all,

Make no mistake.

I compose the song.

And

I hold the tune,

And

I belt it out.

I'm their Saint-Saëns, their Mozart,

   their Elton John, their Shirley Bassey,

Their Dolly Parton – my favourite.

The others, they just play along, sing along,

Yelp along, belch along, whoop and whistle along.

No heavenly chorus,

That's for sure.

Those others out there in these poems –

Don't tell 'em I said –

They're nowt but my droning back-up group,

My caterwauling choir,

My motley band.

But they're all I've got.
With them I have to make
All the music of the earth,
Dawn to dusk
Every day.
Hard graft, I'm telling you.

And you down there, you in the hat,
Writing this stuff,
You're no Shakespeare, are you?
What do you go and do?
You leave me till last.
That wasn't kind, not polite,
Not right,
Not fair.
But I know why – don't worry.
I'm not flash; I'm not rare,
Not endangered,
Yet.

I'm ordinary enough – I know that –
Common in your garden.
"Just that blackbird again,"
I hear you say.
Yet,
Every morning, of every day,
I sing for you,
In your park,
From your rooftop,
In your tree.
You hardly notice I'm there,
That I'm me.

But I'm the one that starts the song,
That makes the music,
That makes the carnival,
The carnival of animals,
Not them,
Not you,
Poet man.

There, I've had the last word.
I am Blackbird.

The End